Mrs Vole the Vet

Ahlberg & Chichester Clark

PUFFIN

PUFFIN BOOKS

UK | USA | Canada | Ireland | Australia
India | New Zealand | South Africa

Puffin Books is part of the Penguin Random House group of companies
whose addresses can be found at global.penguinrandomhouse.com.

www.penguin.co.uk   www.puffin.co.uk   www.ladybird.co.uk

First published in hardback by Viking and in paperback by Puffin Books 1996
This edition published 2016

001

Printed in China
A CIP catalogue record for this book is available from the British Library

ISBN: 978–0–141–37483–3

All correspondence to:
Puffin Books, Penguin Random House Children's
80 Strand, London WC2R 0RL

Meet Mrs Vole the vet.
Mrs Vole has one son,
two daughters,
three cats,
four dogs
and *no* husband.

Mr Vole has three stepsons,
eleven rabbits
and a new wife.
We will forget about him.

Mrs Vole works hard.

She works day and night,

week after week

and all the year round.

No job is too little.

No job is too big.

No job is too fast,

too slow,

or too low.

. . . high.

No job is too . . .

Mrs Vole is worn out.
She comes home from work
and falls asleep in a chair.

Her children make the tea,
put her slippers on –
and worry about her.

"What you need is a *boyfriend*, Mum," they say.
"Hm," says Mrs Vole.
She sips her tea. "Do you think so?"
"Yes!"
"What sort of boyfriend?"
"A nice one!" the children yell.
"With a nice smile!"
"A nice wallet!"
"And nice football boots!"

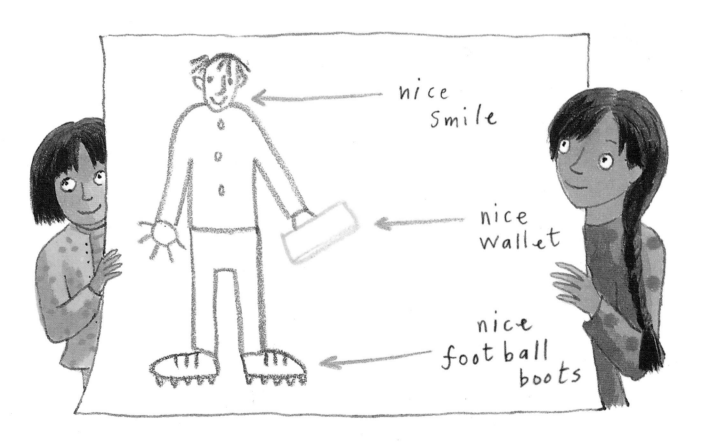

And Mrs Vole thinks, "Hm."

A few days later, Mrs Vole meets
Mr Lamp the lighthouse keeper.

Mr Lamp has a nice smile,
a nice cat
and a nice lighthouse.

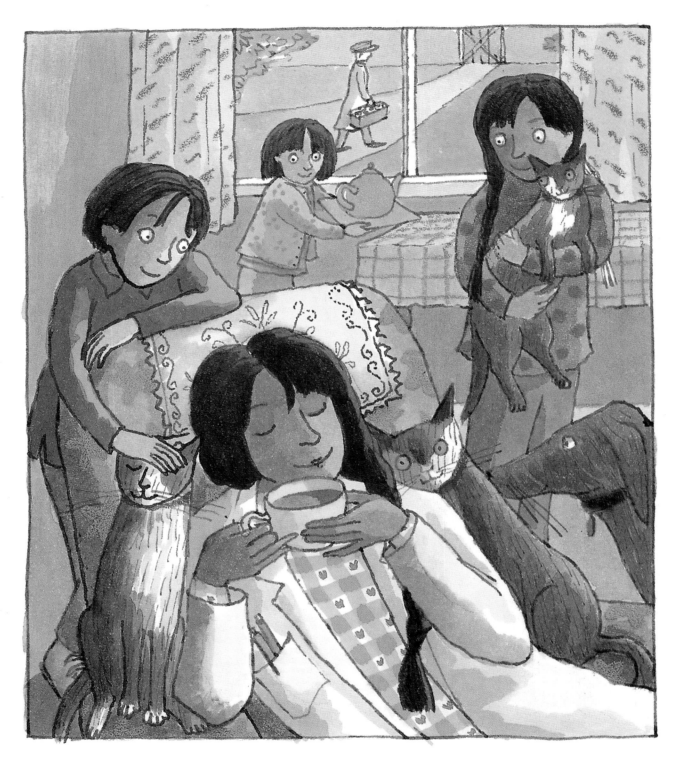

"He's not bad, Mum," the children say.

"Hm," says Mrs Vole.

She sips her tea. "The only trouble is . . .

. . . TOO MANY STEPS!"

"OK," the children say.
"We will forget about him."

A few days later, Mrs Vole meets
Mr Field the farmer.

Mr Field has a nice smile, a nice truck,

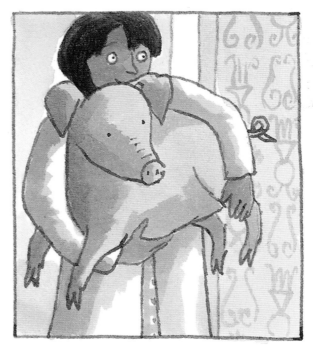

a very nice cheque book and a poorly pig.

"*He's* not bad, Mum," the children say.
"Hm," says Mrs Vole.
"Do you think so?"
"Yes!"

"Lovely cheque book!"
"Lovely pig!"
"Hm," says Mrs Vole.
She sips her tea. "The only trouble is . . .

. . . A HUNDRED AND FIFTY OTHER PIGS!"

"Phew!" the children say.
"We will forget about *him*."

Mrs Vole goes back to work.
She works seven days a week.
She works seven nights a week.

No job is too big.   No job is too little.

No job is too wet,   too spotty,

or too complicated.   No job is too rude.

Mrs Vole is worn out.
She comes home from work
and falls asleep at the table.
Her children make the breakfast,
put her slippers on –
and worry about her.

"What you *really* need
is a boyfriend, Mum," they say.
"Hm," says Mrs Vole.
She eats her cornflakes.
"Do you think so?"

A few weeks later, Mrs Vole meets:

Mr Shout the sergeant.
"Too bossy!"

Mr Green the grocer.
"Too cabbagy!"

Mr Aaargh! the actor.
"Too embarrassing!"

Aaargh!

"OK," the children say.
"We will forget about *them*."

Then, one morning the doorbell rings.
On the step stands a man
in a nice white coat.
He has a nice smile on his face
and a poorly pigeon in his hands.

Meet Mr Moo the milkman.
"Hallo, there!"

Mrs Vole takes care of the pigeon.
The children take care of the milkman.

When Mr Moo leaves,
the children rush up to their mum.
"*He's* not bad, Mum."
"Do you think so?"
"Yes!" the children yell.
"No steps!"
"No pigs!"
"No shouting!"
"You might be right," says Mrs Vole.
"The only trouble is . . .

. . . MRS MOO!"

A few days later,
Mrs Vole and the children
make a picnic
and drive off to the seaside.

The sun is shining.
The sand is warm.
The waves are splashing on the rocks.

Mrs Vole is smiling
as she climbs the *lighthouse* stairs.

"After all," she thinks.
"What's a few steps . . .

. . . between friends."

The End